Hal Knows Martial Arts

Vickie Erickson

Illustrated by Avery Liell-Kok

Kamsahamnida
Vickie J Erickson
6-10-19

AuthorHouse™ LLC
1663 Liberty Drive
Bloomington, IN 47403
www.authorhouse.com
Phone: 1-800-839-8640

Published by AuthorHouse 12/14/2013

ISBN: 978-1-4918-4138-9 (sc)
ISBN: 978-1-4918-4142-6 (e)

Library of Congress Control Number: 2013922821

authorHOUSE®

To my husband, Tim, and our four children, Austin, Billie, Taylor, and Holden. Thank you for the encouragement and support!

School problems

"Hello, Tony! How are you today?" I asked as he came running toward me on the playground. I quickly jumped out of the way before he tackled me to the ground. Instead of me falling, Tony did a summersault. "Hey, Tony, what are you doing?" I asked.

He stood up, and looking a little confused he asked, "How did you move away from me so fast?"

I slyly said, "Hmmm, it must be my ninja-like moves I've been working on in class. So why are you running so fast this morning? Do you have something to tell me?"

Tony shook his head no. "I just was happy to see you. What do you want to play?"

But just as I was going to say, "Let's play tag," the bell rang for school.

Tony looked bummed and said, "Well, Hal, I'll see you at lunch. Then let's play at recess."

I smiled and said, "Sure! How about we play tag at recess?" He looked around to see if anyone was listening to us, like he was a super spy, and then nodded yes.

We went to our classrooms, and it seemed like it would be forever until lunch and recess. But then Mr. Manson told us our test time in the computer lab got moved up to the morning. The whole class groaned with disappointment until he said, "Class, if we get the testing done this morning, then we'll have some extra time to play outside this afternoon. Now doesn't that sound like a good idea?" We all looked at one another and agreed that would be fun.

Off we went to the computer lab. I sure hoped it wouldn't be a long test. There were rules in there, such as eyes on your own computer, be quiet, feet flat on the floor, and there were other rules too, but I forgot them.

The test wasn't that hard, and I thought I did well. When some of us got done before the others, we got to play games online.

Finally it was lunchtime. I was saving seats for Tony, Skyler, and Manny. We always sat next to each other and talked about our day, and then we played together at recess. Today we were having spaghetti with breadsticks, green beans, and ice cream. Yummy! I saw Skyler and Manny coming, but I didn't see Tony. Manny was in Tony's class. He said, "Mrs. Collins took Tony to see the principal."

What? How could this be? I thought. Tony doesn't do anything wrong. He's a good kid and gets straight A's all the time.

Finally, Tony came walking over to the table and sat down. I asked him what was going on, but he didn't want to talk about it. Tony is my best friend, and I knew that when he was ready to talk, he'd let me know.

Skyler asked, "Well, Hal, are you ready for tomorrow?" I think I must have looked a little confused. "Are you ready for the promotion?" he asked.

"Oh, I almost forgot about the promotion at martial arts. Yes, I think I remember everything. Too bad you aren't testing with me this time, Skyler."

"Hal, do you want to go over the forms at recess today?" I looked at him with a mouthful of spaghetti and nodded my head yes. Then I looked at Tony and remembered we were going to play tag. I quickly finished my spaghetti and said, "Skyler, could we do the forms one time? And then we'll all play tag together. Would that be okay, Tony?"

He just shrugged his shoulders and said, "That would be fine. I really wish my parents would let me join martial arts classes." We all finished eating so we could go play. I felt bad for Tony. He wanted to be in martial arts, but his parents didn't think it would be good for him.

"Tony, are you sure it's okay?" I asked him.

"Yeah, it's fine. I need some time to think for a little bit, so I'll sit here and watch." Tony sat by the big tree in the green grass.

"Okay, if you're sure. Tony, if you want to talk, let me know. You're my best friend!"

Tony looked up and said, "I know we're best friends. I'll be fine. Besides, it's not going to take you too long."

Skyler was waiting for me, and Manny decided to go swing. He was going so high in the air that he looked like he was flying with the birds. Skyler said, "Hal, I know you know martial arts, so are you ready?"

Without any hesitation, I said, "Absolutely, Skyler! Let's do this!" When we practice at school, we said "Hiya" quietly. We both thought we made it through the four forms in record time. "Skyler, the only thing I get confused about is my stances with my kicks and blocks." Skyler said he also got confused by them. Well, now we both knew we weren't alone with that.

"Okay, who wants to play tag?" I asked.

Tony, Manny, and Skyler jumped up, running and yelling, "You're it!"

Before long, the bell rang, and I saw Tony walking to the door instead of running. I said to him, "See you on the bus ride home." He nodded okay.

On the ride home, Tony was so quiet, which was not like him. I just talked about my day and said that I needed to find my uniform and belt, even though I knew exactly where they were. I asked, "Do you want to come over for a snack at my house today?"

"No, I'll pass today. I have chores and homework to get done," he said.

"Tony, you do know it's Friday, right? And you have all weekend to get your homework done."

He nodded and then said, "Hey, good luck tomorrow with your promotion." I asked him if he wanted to come and watch, but I knew the answer to that. His parents thought that he would get hurt. Tony just kept walking and waved bye.

When I walked in the house, Mom said, "Hi, Hal! How was school today?"

After thinking for a moment, I replied, "It was good to start, but I'm worried about Tony. He just hasn't been himself since I saw him at lunch. Manny said that Mrs. Collins took Tony to the principal's office."

Mom said, "Well that isn't like Tony to be sent to the principal, so something must have happened after you saw him this morning. Did he tell you anything?"

I looked up at her and shook my head no. "Mom, I told Tony that if he wanted to talk to me, he could."

She said, "Hal, that was very thoughtful of you, and when he's ready, I bet he will let you know."

I took a fresh chocolate chip cookie and got a glass of milk for my snack. "Hey, Mom, do you think Tony's parents will ever let him come watch one of my promotions?" She just shrugged her shoulders and raised her hands.

"Hal, are you all ready for the promotion in the morning?"

"Yes, Mom."

"Do you remember everything?" Mom asked me.

"I just have trouble remembering my stances with my kicks and blocks." I finished my snack and said, "Mom, can I go play with Aaron for a little bit?"

"I'll give you two hours. All right? Then you'll go through the sayings and definitions?" I nodded yes. I went to play with my big brother, Aaron, on the video games. And besides, if I needed help with my blocks and kicks, I could always ask Aaron, since he is a martial arts instructor.

Right around suppertime, Dad got home. We all chatted about our day and what we were doing for the weekend and where I wanted to go for lunch on my birthday, this Sunday. Then Mom said, "Hal, are you ready to practice your sayings and definitions?" I wanted to say no, but I knew better than to argue with my mom. So I agreed to go through the sayings with her.

Aaron said, "Should I go through the block and kick patterns with you? Then we can go through the forms one time each before I go pick up Ann to go to the movies."

I turned around, looked at him, and said, "Aaron, you would do that for me? But I think I know what I'm doing."

Aaron said, "Okay, smarty pants, then you can prove it to me after you're done with Mom's test!"

Mom sent the girls to watch a movie with Dad in the living room, and we practiced. She would say a word like "aph chagi," and then I would tell her what it meant. "Aph chagi means front snap kick," I said.

"How about kamsahamnida?"

That's an easy one, but it was hard to learn to say at first. "It means thank you."

"All right, Mr. Know It All, then how high can you count in Korean? Shijak!" I started to chuckle a bit when she said shijak, which means to begin.

I started counting, "*Hana, dool, set, net, tasot, yosot, ilgope, yadul, ahope, yol* ..."

Mom put her hands up to stop me. "All right, you've got the counting down all the way up to thirty. Good job! What does *dojang* mean?"

"It means training hall, Mom. Can we be done now?" I asked her. She said yes.

Aaron was still waiting for me in the basement. Well, I did need help, as I kept getting my feet mixed up, as well as my left from my right. He taught me a trick about the left and right. He said, "Hal, hold up your hands in front of you, palms facing away from you. Now look at your thumbs when you hold all your fingers together and point your thumbs toward each other like this." I looked at Aaron to see how he was doing it. "When you do this and look at your left hand, you will see the letter L, so this is your left hand."

"Cool! Why has no one taught this to me sooner, Aaron?" I gave Aaron a high five.

"See you tomorrow, and, Hal, you can do it. *Pil sung!*"

I went to watch the movie with Dad, Bella, Trista, and Mom. They were watching a comedy about three kids pulling pranks on their parents during vacation, but I still couldn't help worrying about Tony.

Promotion Day

As we were on our way to Emerald, we drove by a river and a lake, and I just couldn't help wondering why Tony's parents didn't like martial arts. There was a sailboat race going on. I wished we had time to watch. When we got to the academy, there were lots of cars.

On the way into the building, Bella decided she really didn't want to be here. Dad and Mom pulled her aside and told her to behave. After all, she is fourteen years old. My sister was trying to convince Mom and Dad that she didn't like martial arts. The worst thing was she is really good at it. She has trophies and ribbons, and she is a brown belt student.

Trista, my other sister, is twelve years old, and she's a blue belt student. Trista loved getting dressed up in the uniform. She's more like Aaron. She is laid back, loves to help with special events at schools, and teach others about the sport of martial arts, especially all the little kids. The only problem was she didn't care if she was promoted or not. She was waiting for either Mom or Dad to start going to classes with her again. Dad was a green stripe belt student, but he didn't have the time for class with his work schedule, and Mom is a brown stripe belt student, and she just got really busy with work too.

As I looked through the windows, I saw lots of people in the *dojang*, more than ever before. I turned to Aaron and asked, "Do you know how many are promoting, Aaron?" He didn't know.

"Hello, ma'am," I said as I ninja-walked very quietly into the building.

Mrs. Garcia turned around and said, "Hello, sir. How are you today?"

"I'm great today, ma'am, because I get to come here, and it's my birthday tomorrow too!"

She said, "Well, happy early birthday, sir. How old will you be tomorrow?"

I looked at Mrs. Garcia and told her, "I'll officially be eleven, ma'am."

She smiled and said, "Well, congratulations! You better hurry and get ready for the promotion, sir." She turned and said, "Mr. & Mrs. Johnson, hello! How are you today?" As I was walking away, I could hear them talking, and I saw Bella pouting in the corner. I just rolled my eyes at her. Trista was busy reading her books already.

As I entered the *dojang*, I bowed at the door before entering and again before walking onto the giant blue mat. It smelled clean in there, like fresh rain, not like sweat from Wednesday night. That night, it was hot and sticky in there, and everyone was so sweaty.

Everyone was dressed in their nice, clean uniforms and ready for the promotion. But first we needed to practice our forms, so I asked if Tammy and Danny would like to practice with me. Tammy was upset. "Are you okay?" I asked her.

Tammy said, "No, I don't want to be here. My parents are making me do this."

I asked, "What's more important than this promotion?"

Tammy said, "I never wanted to be in martial arts, but my parents told me it would be a good, fun sport. They also said it would help me make friends and teach me to defend myself."

"But, Tammy, I've seen you make lots of friends at school, and you're really good at martial arts. Also, martial arts is a good way to learn to defend yourself in case you ever need to. Why would you not want to be here?"

She couldn't come up with a reason. Tammy said, "Hal, I didn't think anyone even cared about me. I've made more friends this year, and I'm doing better in school. Do you really think it's because of being here at the academy?"

I smiled at her and said, "Absolutely it is!"

Just then, Mrs. Garcia walked in and said, "Class, time to line up!"

Everyone said, "Yes, ma'am!" We all ran and lined up according to belt rank and stood very still with our hands held tightly in fists in front of us. In the front of the class were twelve of Mrs. Garcia's black belts students ready to test us.

Mrs. Garcia asked, "Are you all ready and excited for the promotion?"

"Yes, ma'am!" we all replied.

She turned and looked at Travis, a blue-stripe student, and told him to bow us in with a pledge. We all repeated after him and then got enough space for jumping jacks, pushups, and sit-ups.

Oh no. I looked over at Danny. He looked a little nervous. I whispered to him, "Danny, take a deep breath. You'll do just fine!" He took a deep breath, and then he relaxed a bit.

We had to show everything we had learned in class to get our next belt. There were a lot of us up on the mat. The *dojang* was starting to get hot with so many people. Our parents were taking pictures of all of us either from the bleachers or up on the mat. During promotions was the only time parents could come up on the mat, as long as they took off their shoes and stood or sat in the corners. Great. I saw Mom taking pictures of Mrs. Garcia. She was a third-degree black belt and really nice. Also, she was taking pictures of Aaron since he was on the testing board again. Aaron's sixteen years old and working on getting his second-degree black belt this year. And, of course Mom is taking pictures of me. My grandma told me I looked a lot like Aaron.

Mrs. Garcia told us what to do and said that if we needed a reminder, she would help us out. Then she said, "Please do ten each of the blocking and striking form with *Kihaps* when you start and end. *Shijak!*"

We finished that, and then she instructed us to do ten front snap kicks on each leg. "*Shijak!*" I was starting to feel a bit sweaty. "Well done, everyone. Next we will do back, side, and front falls from a squatting position. *Shijak!*" I couldn't wait to learn how to do a sky fall like Aaron. Now that I was getting to be a higher rank, I could start doing more fun things. Mrs. Garcia said, "Now that you're all warmed up, time to stretch and count in Korean up to forty, one through ten for the first stretch, eleven through twenty for the next stretch, and so on. *Shijak!*"

After we finished, she said, "Please turn away from the flags and fix your uniforms and then turn back around." We were thankful for the quick break. Now it was time to do our forms. I had four forms to show the testing board that included my older brother, Aaron. We all did the first form together. Then the group testing for their yellow stripe belt sat down, and after that, Mrs. Garcia asked the yellow belt students to have a seat. When the students with their green stripe belts were done with their form, they had to sit down. Next it was time for my group to test for our green belts, and then we sat by the wall. When the students testing for their blue stripe belts were done, they sat by us.

Next was Travis, who did the sixth form all by himself. He was doing great until he forgot a move and got all turned around. "Oh no," I whispered to Jewels, "that's not good."

Mrs. Garcia said, "Mr. Travis Reed, would you like to start this form again?"

Travis said, "Yes, ma'am," and he took a deep breath. Then my big brother, Aaron, asked Mrs. Garcia if he could talk to him quickly and whispered some advice in his ear. Aaron was very good at martial arts, and he had taken first place in the tournaments. I hoped someday I would be as good as my brother, Aaron.

Travis did his form again, and it was awesome! Now Travis had to do a Bo staff form that he made up. He started by introducing himself to the testing board, saying, "Testing board, my name is Travis Reed. I represent the Garcia Martial Arts Academy in Emerald, and with your permission, I will be performing a Bo form for you."

Mr. Swanson asked, "Mr. Reed, have you inspected your weapon?"

Travis said, "Yes, sir. Would you like to take a look at it?"

Mr. Swanson said, "No, thank you. You may get the space you need, sir." Travis backed up to get more room, not turning his back to the testing board. He began by twirling the Bo all around him and yelling "Hiya!" several times as he poked at the air in front and to the side of him. He also stood with the Bo held above his head while balancing on one foot. He also did a figure eight with the Bo staff, which was impressive. Right before he came to attention, he twirled the Bo above his head. That was fantastic. Travis bowed to the black belts and Mrs. Garcia. She said, "Well done, Mr. Reed. Please go put your Bo away. Thank you." Everyone clapped for Travis.

Time to take a deep breath because Danny, Chloe, Jewels, and I had our very first board breaks. Now I was feeling a bit nervous because I had never had so many people watching. When it was my turn, I told the testing board that I would do a palm heel break. Then I set myself up in front of my board holders and did a practice break first. I looked up at them and asked, "Board holders, ready?"

They answered, "Yes, sir!"

I yelled, "Hiya!" and went through the board. I did it!

Now we needed to find a partner and line up. I picked Danny, one of my friends. Now it was time for Judo. This was the fun part of martial arts. I hoped we would get to throw each other today.

Danny was worried he forgot the holds, but I knew what to do. I figured he was just nervous. He said, "Hal, I couldn't have done this promotion without you!" That made me smile from ear to ear!

Time for questions. Mr. Burman called my name first. I stood up, turned away from the flags, fixed my uniform, turned back around, and then said, "Yes, sir!" and bowed.

He said, "Can you translate what a front snap kick is called in Korean?"

I said, "Sir, it is an *ahp chagi.*"

Mr. Burman said, "Very good. Can you tell me what tenet you like the best and why?"

"I like the courtesy tenet because everyone deserves respect, sir."

Then he said, "Very good, Mr. Johnson. You may have a seat on the floor." I sat in the hero's pose while everyone else answered their questions.

Finally, Mrs. Garcia said, "Stand up and shake your legs out. Then find the person who tested you."

Mr. Burman and I met. He said, "Mr. Johnson, sir, you did very well today, and I can't wait to see you in your new belt! Remember to keep all your kicks above your belt level." He also said I was a very good sport for helping Danny when he got nervous and talking to Tammy before the promotion when she was upset.

We shook hands and said, "Kamsahamnida."

Wow, I did it! Now everyone testing lined up on one side of the room facing the flags, and Mrs. Garcia and the black belt students all lined up in a row in front of the flags. She started calling out our names one at a time. We walked over to her and took our new belt. Then we said thank you and shook her hand. We thanked all the black belts, including Aaron, and shook their hands. We walked back to our spots and waited for Mrs. Garcia to say, "Please turn away from the flag and put your new belt on. If anyone needs help putting on their new belt, please ask for help. And if any of you black belts see someone needing help, please offer to help them."

Once we had our new belts on, Mrs. Garcia said, "We have a tradition here at Garcia Martial Arts Academy that is called the Attitude of Gratitude. This is where we take our old belts and present them to someone who has helped us along our journey to get to our new belt. It may be a teacher, another student, your parents, or the person who gets you here for class. Please take your old belt and present it to someone and say thank you."

Obviously, I chose my mom *because* if she hadn't brought me, I would not have *been* there having fun with all my new friends, and I would not have had the confidence that I now did.

Surprise, surprise, Danny chose me to give his belt to. He said, "Hal, thank you for all of your help. You are a terrific friend!" I felt very special.

Then, guess who came over next? Tammy! She said, "Thank you for the encouragement, and I know you know martial arts too, Hal. You keep it up, and I bet you'll be passing me up in belts soon."

"Class, time to bow out, and then we'll take a group photo of everyone," said Mrs. Garcia. We bowed out, shook everyone's hands, and took pictures. Even some goofy pictures.

After I changed out of my uniform, Mrs. Garcia and Mr. Burman asked to speak to me for a moment. I went with them, and they said, "Mr. Hal Johnson, you know your martial arts, and we would like you to start training with the weapons in your next class."

Wow, I couldn't believe it! "This was the best promotion ever!" I told them. They also said that I would be training with my big brother, Aaron, Travis, Tammy, Danny, Skyler, and Jewels, which made me even happier.

Aaron came walking around the corner and said, "Congratulations, Hal! I knew you could do it, little buddy!" I couldn't wait to tell my mom and dad the good news!

Dad asked Danny and his parents if they wanted to meet us at the Mexican restaurant to eat with us and help us celebrate our new belts and my birthday. They said, "Yes, that sounds like fun!"

What I didn't know was that they planned a surprise party for me there with my martial arts friends. We also all got fried ice cream for dessert, and it was delicious! Then we went to a movie at the theatre called *Super Ninja Kid*! It was a great weekend.

School on Monday

On Monday at school, I found my best friend, Tony, standing by his locker, and he asked me, "How was the promotion? Did you get your new belt, Hal?"

As I was getting ready to tell him about the promotion, he became very quiet and looked almost scared. Then I felt heavy breathing on my neck. When I turned around, there was the school bully. He stood so close to me that I could smell his breath. I took a step to the side and casually said, "Hey, Brady, how's it going today?"

Brady just looked at me and said not to talk to him because he wanted to talk with Tony. He looked at me and then at Tony and said, "You can't hide from me, Tony. I know all the classes you're in. And you, Hal, don't you say a word to anyone, or you're next." Then he punched Tony right in the stomach and walked away.

I helped Tony up from the ground. He was trying not to cry, but it looked like it hurt. "Tony, why did Brady do that? What's going on?" Tony just told me to let it be, but I couldn't. After all, he's my best friend, and everyone was scared of Brady. Tony begged me not to say anything to the teachers. I agreed for now, but I wanted to find out why Brady was being so mean to Tony.

At lunch, I sat by Tony and asked again. He leaned over the table and whispered to me, "Brady got caught cheating on our test Friday in Mrs. Collins's class. He was copying off my paper."

"So why did he punch you if he was the one cheating?" I asked.

"Well because he thinks I set him up, but I didn't know he had been copying off my papers. We both got sent down to Mr. William's office. When we came out of Principal William's office, Brady was mad at me and said he was going to make me pay for it."

"But it's not your fault he cheated." Then who shows up but Brady. He told Tony and me that we had to be his friends or else.

"No way, Brady. I will not be your friend, and neither will Tony! So leave us alone."

Brady was a scary kid. He looked at me and said, "Hal, you're going to pay for this!"

Just then, the bell rang for class. We didn't even realize we sat in the cafeteria eating through all of recess. I had gym class, and Tony had Math. My lucky day. Brady had the same class as me. Today we were playing soccer. When I got the ball, Brady was yelling at me to kick it to him, but I didn't need to, so I kicked it in the goal. We went to get a drink of water, and Brady pushed me down to the ground, saying it was his soccer ball to kick in the goal. I said, "Brady, it's a game, and I was closer to the goal than you. What's your problem anyway?"

"You! You're my problem, so you better watch out or I'll beat you up, Hal!"

At the end of the day, Tony came to my house. We needed to figure out what to do with Brady. During the whole ride, we brainstormed, trying to decide what to do. I thought of an idea. "Tony, you need to learn how to protect yourself from Brady. I can teach you some martial arts moves, and then maybe he won't bother you anymore."

"That's a great idea, Hal, but when are you going to have the time to teach me?"

I nodded. "Okay, new plan. Maybe you should join martial arts."

Tony thought about it but remembered what his parents told him. He said, "My mom and dad won't go for that. They think it will teach me to be mean, and they don't want me to get hurt. I think it would be fun. Maybe you should just be my bodyguard."

I said, "But, Tony, we don't have all the same classes together, so that would be difficult. Maybe we should talk to our parents about it. What do you think?" Tony shook his head no and said "that would be the worst thing to do." He made me promise to not tell anyone, even my parents. I reluctantly agreed with one condition, that if Brady went after us again, I would tell on him. Tony agreed and then walked over to his house.

Where's Tony?

The next morning, I couldn't find Tony anywhere at school. I started to worry about him. Out of the corner of my eye, I saw Brady walking toward me, so I took off walking faster for the classroom. After all, I didn't want to talk to him or be his friend. But he caught me and cornered me in the hall where there weren't any cameras and got right in my face and asked, "Where is Tony?"

I said, "I don't know where Tony is. Why do you need him?"

He said, "Hal, it's none of your business, but he has something of mine, and I need it back." What could Tony have of Brady's? And why wasn't Tony at school?

When I got home from school, I walked in the house and told Mom I had to go to Tony's house to see if he was okay. But she said we didn't have time and that we needed to get to martial arts class. So I asked if I could call over there, and she said to be quick. There was no answer, so I decided I'd have to try again later.

We arrived at martial arts, and Aaron was already in class teaching the kids younger than me. Then I had an idea. I would talk to Aaron later to see if he could help me teach Tony how to protect himself from Brady. That would work. Now I felt better!

Class was fun. I got my new nunchucks in class. The mat-chat topic was about how to handle bullies. Did they know something was going on and decided to talk about it? I wondered. While I sat there listening, I knew I had to do something to help Tony out of the trouble with Brady. So I decided that he needed to pick on someone his own size, more like me. After all, I did know some martial arts moves.

Mrs. Garcia said, "The best way to deal with a bully is not to fight, because they are trying to intimidate you, and if you stand up to them, they usually back down. And sometimes the bully wants to fight because they want someone to feel pain. But the most important thing to do if someone is being bullied is to talk to an adult. It could be your parents, a teacher, principal, counselor, or police officer." Then she asked, "What do bullies do to kids?"

Our answers were, "They hit, tease, trip, push, pull, punch, kick, call you names, and throw things at you."

So she said, "Why do they do that?" We all thought about that. Hmmm, now that was a good question. I'd have to think about that.

The Plan

When we got home, I went to Tony's house and asked his mom if I could talk to him. She said, "Sure." I went to his room, and he was sitting at his desk doing homework.

"Hal, what are you doing here?" Tony looked tired.

I asked, "Why weren't you at school today?" He said he had lots of homework to do, and he wasn't feeling good. "Tony, were you scared to go to school today because of Brady?" I asked him. He tried to deny it, but I could tell he was scared of him. "What if I tell you I have a plan to get him to leave us alone? Would that help you?"

Tony looked up, kind of curious now about what I was thinking, and said, "Maybe. What are you thinking, Hal?"

"Okay, are you ready for this? We're going to find out why he's being mean to you. I know why he's mean to me. That was easy to figure out. Now, Tony, have you ever told him I go to martial arts?" I asked Tony this because I don't brag about being in martial arts to others.

He thought for a moment and said, "I don't think I've told anybody that other than my parents. How are you going to find out why he's being mean to me?"

I looked at Tony and said, "Brady said you have something of his. What do you have of his that he was looking for today?"

Tony looked at the floor and said quietly, "He was looking for this, his homework, and he wanted me to give him my iPod. So I thought if I didn't go to school today, he would forget about it." Tony looked really sad now and not sure what to do.

"Tony, why are you doing his homework for him and why does he want your iPod?"

"Brady said if I didn't do his homework for him, he would beat me up since he got caught cheating on the test, and he wants my iPod to keep me from telling anyone." As I was thinking about this, it just didn't make any sense. After all, Brady was twelve years old. He was held back a year in school. He should have been able to do his own homework, and yeah, I knew not everyone liked homework, but it wasn't fair to have someone else do it, let alone take their iPod.

"All right, Tony, here's my plan. Give me his homework. I'm going to do it for him and somehow get him to turn it into Mrs. Collins. You tell Brady that I did his homework."

"Gee, I don't know about this, Hal. This sounds like we're both going to get beat up."

As I was thinking to myself, it dawned on me what to do next. "Tony, just do it, and then tell him you know where to find me under the light by the side door, and if he says something about the camera, just say everyone knows that camera doesn't work, and that's why they hang out there." Tony thought about it and finally agreed to hand me the homework.

I looked at him and said, "Just trust me. You're not going to lose your iPod either, and Brady won't be bothering us anymore after tomorrow. I promise, Tony. I'll see you at school in the morning. And, Tony, remember it only takes thirty seconds of courage! You can do it."

When I got home, I erased most of the answers and filled in random answers. *There, this should be good.* Then it was supper time, and there was nothing unusual to talk about. Well I probably should have, but I needed my plan to work. So I kept it to myself. Mom asked what I found out from Tony. I said, "I guess he wasn't feeling good, and he stayed home to rest."

After supper, I got my own homework done and put it in my backpack with Brady's. I called Manny and Skyler and asked if they could meet Tony and me in the entry at school in the morning. I told them about my plan and asked if they would help. I just had one more detail to work out, and I needed Aaron's help for that in case Brady tried to fight me. Then I needed a good night's sleep so I was prepared for the morning.

Homework Done

When Tony and I walked into school, Skyler and Manny were waiting for us. We all walked to Mrs. Collins's room and chatted in there until Brady showed up. Tony got Mrs. Collins's attention away from the desks. I saw Brady coming in and quickly put his homework on Tony's desk so he would see it. He walked by and looked down and saw his name on the papers. Manny asked Skyler, Tony, and me if we wanted to go outside. "Sure, Manny, let's go."

As we were walking out, I saw Brady grab the papers, and I heard him say, "Mrs. Collins, here is my homework I forgot yesterday."

She took it and looked at it and said, "You did this, Brady?" He nodded his head yes. "Are you sure? Because this doesn't look like your handwriting, Brady." Their voices were trailing off as we walked away.

"Time for the next step. Tony, are you ready? Just remember what I said about the light and broken camera. Okay?" Tony nodded, and I walked over to the side door and waited. What Tony didn't know was that I had sent Skyler and Manny to talk to Mr. Williams so he could watch the camera.

Right on time. Brady was following Tony and said, "What did you do to my homework? Mrs. Collins is asking me if I did it."

Tony must have remembered what I said about the thirty seconds of courage because he said, "Well, actually I didn't do it, Brady. Hal did it for you. If you want to talk to him, he's over by the side door by the light waiting for you."

Brady looked really mad now and said, "There's a camera there! I'm not going over there, you idiot."

I could see Tony was getting nervous, and then I heard him say, "There are teachers around us here, and everyone here knows that camera hasn't worked for a while now."

Brady said, "You're coming with me. Let's go before I beat both you and Hal up."

They soon arrived. "Hey, Hal, what do you think you're doing with my homework?" Brady barked at me.

"Well, I thought I was helping out, Tony. Sorry, I won't do it again. Hey how about you do your own homework, Brady? Now that's an idea," I said to him.

"Oh, you're trying to be smart with me now. I'll teach you a thing or two about that!" Brady said, and he shoved Tony toward the ground. I caught him before he fell down. Tony quickly moved out of the way. Brady was mad.

I looked at him and said, "Why can't you do your own work? And why are you bullying Tony?"

He replied, "None of your business! This is between Tony and me, not you!"

"See, that's where you're wrong. I'm Tony's friend and not yours. I don't like people being mean to my friends. So leave us alone before I tell on you. I don't want to fight you, and neither does Tony." We started to walk away, but Brady grabbed me by my collar. I told him, "Let me go, Brady. I don't want to hurt you." He just laughed in my face. Then he pushed me toward the building, and out of the corner of my eye, I could see Skyler, Manny, and Mr. Williams walking toward us. Brady still wouldn't let go and then decided to punch me. That was when he loosened his grip, and my martial arts training came in handy. I escaped his grip and ducked. He punched the brick wall and fell to the ground crying. I think he might have broken his hand.

I bent down to him and said, "Brady, I am a martial artist, and it is on camera what you did. I think Mr. Williams, the principal, wants to talk to you now. Good luck!"

Mr. Williams stopped Tony and me and asked if we were okay. We looked at each other and said, "Yes, we're fine, but Brady might need help." He said he would deal with Brady and would talk to us later. We said okay and looked around and saw the

kids all looking at us. We walked away with Skyler and Manny as the bell rang for classes to start.

"Hal, that was so awesome! How did you know to do that?" Tony asked.

"Well, see here, Tony, I called Skyler and Manny last night and told them about my plan for Brady. Aaron also helped out too. He told me we needed to let Mr. Williams know what was going on. That's why he came walking out when he did with Skyler and Manny. But even if he hadn't come out when he did, the camera was still there, and Skyler was coming to help talk down Brady too. Bullies don't like to be around a crowd of people, we learned." Tony was very happy we helped him.

Right before lunch, Mr. Williams called Tony, Skyler, Manny, and me to his office. I asked if I could talk to him first to explain what was going on, but he said he really needed to talk to all of us. I looked at Tony, and he actually looked relaxed.

We all told our story to Mr. Williams, and he said, "Hal, you are a good friend, and what you have learned at the martial arts academy actually helped you figure out how to help Tony. I know Brady will not be bothering any of you again." He also said, "You should have talked to your teachers, parents, or me about Brady." He went onto say that Brady had a week's worth of reflection time in the office, and he needed to redo tests. His parents were also called about him cheating and fighting. Then Mr. Williams thanked Skyler and Manny for helping to solve the problem with Brady.

"But, Mr. Williams, I have one question. why was Brady making Tony do his homework for him and then cheating off his tests?"

He said, "See, Hal, Brady has a rough home life and thinks that yelling or making someone else do his work is okay because that's what has happened to him. That's why he thought he could bully Tony into doing all his homework for him. There are bullies who like to pick on others who are smarter or different than they are or for no reason at all. Or they pick on kids that have trouble sticking up for themselves or are more sensitive than others. So Brady wanted Tony's iPod as payment that he wouldn't say anything to anyone. This just helped him feel more important. But if you hadn't been so persistent with Tony, we wouldn't know that Brady was having problems at home. So thank you for caring about your friend."

The Rest of the Day

What a day. I felt great, and kids were coming up to me and thanking me for what I did! It made me feel like I was a superhero or something. But I couldn't wait to go to martial arts and tell Mrs. Garcia all about it. She was the one who made me think really hard about how to solve this problem with Brady and my friend Tony.

The principal did call Tony's Mom and told her everything that was going on. Then he explained how I came up with the plan to get Brady to leave Tony alone. He also explained about the martial arts academy and how Skyler and Manny helped out.

When I got home, I told Mom and Aaron all about my day. Aaron said it was a good idea to have Skyler and Manny talk to the principal. Mom was surprised I kept all this from her and that I didn't even get in trouble at school. I ate my snack and asked if we could get going to martial arts.

Mom said, "Well, let's go then." The whole twenty-minute trip, I smiled about the day and how courageous and brave I was. The best part was that I didn't have to fight Brady, and I helped my best friend, Tony.

When we pulled up to the martial arts building, I jumped out, grabbed my gear, and ran inside to get ready for class. It was Mr. Burman teaching today; he said Mrs. Garcia was in a meeting but would be in soon. We bowed in and started class. I was working on my new form and learning the sky fall. Then Mr. Burman asked us all to line back up to do partner drills. That was when Mrs. Garcia came in and said, "Class, can I have your attention? I would like you to meet our newest student, Mr. Tony Taylor."

I turned around, and there was my best friend and his mom. Tony was wearing a new white martial arts uniform. I couldn't help myself and ran over to him and gave him a great, big hug. I said, "Welcome to Garcia Martial Arts Academy, Tony!"

Mrs. Taylor asked if I could talk to her for a minute. I nodded my head yes, and we walked out to the meeting room. I looked at her and said, "Sorry I didn't tell you about Tony being bullied, Mrs. Taylor, but I didn't want to break a promise to Tony."

She said, "Hal, I'm not upset with you. Actually, I'm very proud that you're Tony's best friend. Because of what you did and how Mr. Williams told me about how you saved Tony from being beaten up, I decided that maybe martial arts is a good thing. So I called your mom, and she told me how well you're doing and gave me the info to come meet with Mrs. Garcia this afternoon before Tony got home. So this is a surprise for both of you! Thank you for being such a terrific friend to Tony, and I know someday he will repay the favor to you!"

About the Author

Vickie Erickson is a stay-at-home wife and mother to four children. She got interested in martial arts when her oldest son joined the local Martial Arts Academy. About three months later, the rest of her family also joined the academy. Over the years, she has also helped with special events for the Martial Arts Academy. She has been a volunteer at the school district her children attend, where she goes in and listens to children read books to her in the elementary classes as well as being a substitute teacher's aide. She has observed the children dealing with different situations at school, home, church and at the academy. She lives in Centuria, Wisconsin, with her husband and children.

CPSIA information can be obtained
at www.ICGtesting.com
Printed in the USA
LVXC01n0717160314
377510LV00002B/28